Superstars
on ice

★ ★ ★ ★ PATTY CRANSTON ★ ★ ★ ★

Kids Can Press Ltd.

To Dandy and Dappy

First U.S. edition 1997

Published in the U.S. by
Kids Can Press Ltd.
85 River Rock Drive, Suite 202
Buffalo, NY 14207

Published in Canada by
Kids Can Press Ltd.
29 Birch Avenue
Toronto, ON M4V 1E2

Edited by Elizabeth MacLeod
Printed in Hong Kong

97 0 9 8 7 6 5 4 3 2 1

Canadian Cataloguing in Publication Data

Cranston, Patty
    Superstars on ice: figure skating champions

U.S. ed.
ISBN 1-55074-400-3

1. Skaters — Biography — Juvenile literature. I. Title.
GV850.A2C73 1997   j796.912'0922   C97-930654-X

Photo credits

Dick Button Collection: 25 (top). **Canada's Sports Hall of Fame:** 16 (all), 17 (all). **Gérard Châtaigneau:** 3 (top), 4 (right), 9 (left), 10 (right), 19 (top), 26 (left), 31 (right), 37 (left). **Thom Hayim:** 37 (middle). **Heiss-Jenkins Private Collection:** 24 (bottom), 25 (bottom right). **Holiday Studio:** 36, 37 (right). **Jenkins Private Collection:** 25 (bottom left). **Barb McCutcheon:** cover (top right), 5 (bottom left), 6 (both), 11 (middle), 12, 13 (all), 14 (both), 15 (all), 22 (top right), 26 (right), 27 (right), 30, 31 (top left), 32 (left, right), 33 (middle), 34 (left), back cover (middle and bottom left). **Rodnina Collection:** 28 (right). **Cam Silverson:** cover (middle, top and bottom left, bottom right), 3 (second from top, second from bottom, bottom), 4 (left), 5 (top left, right), 7 (all), 8 (both), 9 (right), 11 (left, right), 18 (both), 19 (bottom), 22 (left, bottom right), 23 (both), 27 (left, middle), 29 (right), 31 (bottom left), 32 (middle), 33 (left, right), 34 (right), 35 (both), 38 (both), 39 (both), 40 (both), back cover (top left; top, middle and bottom right). **Margaret S. Williamson:** 10 (left), 20, 21 (both), 24 (top), 29 (left). **World Figure Skating Museum:** 28 (left).

Contents

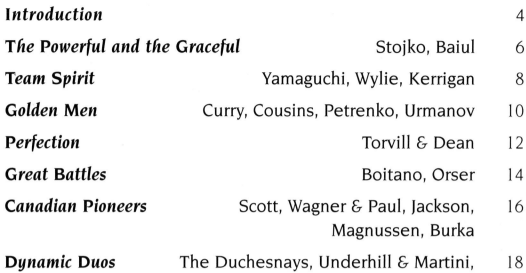

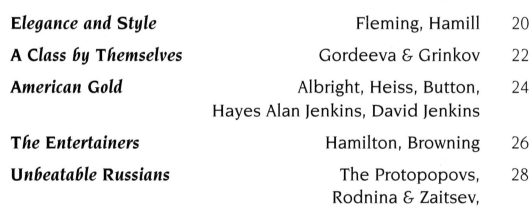

Introduction		4
The Powerful and the Graceful	Stojko, Baiul	6
Team Spirit	Yamaguchi, Wylie, Kerrigan	8
Golden Men	Curry, Cousins, Petrenko, Urmanov	10
Perfection	Torvill & Dean	12
Great Battles	Boitano, Orser	14
Canadian Pioneers	Scott, Wagner & Paul, Jackson, Magnussen, Burka	16
Dynamic Duos	The Duchesnays, Underhill & Martini, Wilson & McCall	18
Elegance and Style	Fleming, Hamill	20
A Class by Themselves	Gordeeva & Grinkov	22
American Gold	Albright, Heiss, Button, Hayes Alan Jenkins, David Jenkins	24
The Entertainers	Hamilton, Browning	26
Unbeatable Russians	The Protopopovs, Rodnina & Zaitsev, Pakhomova & Gorshkov, Bestemianova & Bukin	28
Sizzling Sophistication	Witt	30
Crowd Favorites	Ito, Manley, Candeloro	32
In the Spotlight	Brasseur & Eisler, Klimova & Ponomarenko	34
The Innovator	Cranston	36
Contenders and Defenders	Kwan, Eldredge, Gritschuk & Platov, Meno & Sand	38
The Future	Lipinski, Bourne & Kraatz	40

Thump, thump, thump ...

With her heart pounding, the Olympic figure skater paces backstage as she waits to step onto the ice. Her legs are shaking even though she has competed many times before. "Concentrate and breathe," she tells herself. "And don't rush that triple lutz. Take your time." Meanwhile, her routine is running through her mind, over and over.

Finally — too soon — her name is called, and she glides confidently to center ice. "Just take one section at a time," she reminds herself. "Don't hold back. Attack those jumps!" Throughout her routine, she concentrates only on the move that she is performing, and then she's on to the next. She smiles when she hears the crowd clapping in time to her music.

Four minutes later, it's over. What a relief! And what a fantastic skate. She nailed every jump — even the lutz — and seemed to fly over the ice. "That was the best I've ever skated," she thinks. "This could be my chance for a medal!"

Today, millions of people around the world watch figure skating at arenas and on television. It was the incredible success of Norwegian Sonja Henie, who won three Olympic gold medals from 1928 to 1936, that helped figure skating become the popular sport it is now. Read on and meet other great Olympic skaters — the women, men, pairs and dance teams — who have worked hard for many years to win medals or achieve their place in history by changing the sport forever.

Axel, flip, loop, lutz, salchow, toe loop — these are the various jumps skaters perform. Except for the axel, they all begin with the skater moving backward. Each has a slightly different take-off, and most skaters, including Nancy Kerrigan (right), often find the salchow and toe loop the easiest triples.

The fastest spin is called a corkscrew. It turns at a speed of approximately 10 revolutions/second and 100 km/h (60 m.p.h.). Here's Robin Cousins performing a cross-foot spin, a variation on a corkscrew.

n pairs skating the two skaters not only perform exciting lifts and moves — such as a eath spiral, shown here — as a team, but they must also be able to jump, spin and do ifficult footwork in unison. Isabelle Brasseur and Lloyd Eisler are especially known for kating in perfect time with each other.

ce dancers, such as Jayne orvill and Christopher Dean, ase their routines on ballroom ances. They have to follow strict ules about the type of jumps and lifts llowed in their routines. Another rule ays that dancers aren't allowed to eparate more than five times during heir program.

Kurt Browning has a great triple axel. In this jump the skater is moving forward, then leaps into the air from one leg, rotates three and a half times and lands backward on the other leg, or the "landing leg." The axel is the only jump that takes off when the skater is moving forward, and that gives it an extra half-turn in the air.

The Powerful and the Graceful

Elvis Stojko

 Canada

Olympic Silver, 1994

World Champion, 1994, 1995, 1997

Power is what makes Elvis Stojko a great jumper. He skates with incredible speed to thrust himself high in the air and far across the ice. In competition the "Terminator" is tough to beat because his routines are difficult and exciting. Most experts agree that Stojko has many years of medals in his future.

Unlike some skaters who stretch out their muscles using ballet techniques, Stojko stretches with kung fu and karate exercises. The concentration that Stojko needs for martial arts helps him on the ice, where he became the first man to uncork a quad-triple combination in competition. In a quad-triple, the skater jumps into the air, turns around four times, lands, then quickly goes into a second jump that turns three times in the air.

"Elvis loves a challenge more than anyone I know," says his coach, Doug Leigh. "And he's never satisfied until he gets the best out of himself."

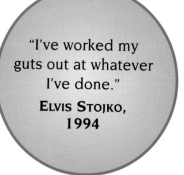

"I've worked my guts out at whatever I've done."
ELVIS STOJKO, 1994

Oksana Baiul

Ukraine

Olympic Champion, 1994

World Champion, 1993

Oksana Baiul is not only one of world's most graceful skaters but she's also a fabulous athlete who can pump out one triple jump after another. The "Ukrainian Jewel" burst upon the skating world at 15 and became one of the youngest skaters ever to win a World Championship. Her skating is smooth and flowing, and her spins are fast and difficult. In one spin, Baiul grabs her skate blade in her hand and has the strength to pull her leg high behind her head as she is spinning.

Baiul's performance at the 1994 Olympics was an amazing show of grit. The day before the finals she gashed her leg and severely injured her back after she crashed with another skater. Baiul was in incredible pain, but she skated like a champion to capture the gold medal. Since then Baiul has had off-ice problems but she's determined to return to top form.

"Usually God forgets to give skaters the soul of an artist. He gave Oksana everything."

GALINA ZMIEVSKAYA, 1993
Baiul's coach

Baiul often talks to her skates before she competes. Sometimes you can also see her bow her head to say a prayer in memory of her mother, who died when Baiul was just 13.

Team Spirit

Kristi Yamaguchi

 U.S.A.

Olympic Champion, 1992

World Champion, 1991, 1992

Her skating is a lovely display of beautiful spins, good triple jumps and graceful movements, but what makes Kristi Yamaguchi soar to the top is her rock-solid consistency. Even under pressure "Yama" looks totally relaxed as she completes one element and moves smoothly on to the next.

Yamaguchi was born with club feet, which means that her feet turned inward instead of pointing straight ahead. To help correct this, Yamaguchi's mother signed her up for skating lessons. Yama loved skating and went on to become not only a talented singles skater but also a top pairs skater. She and her partner, Rudy Galindo, were U.S. Pairs Champions in 1989 and 1990.

"I want to be remembered as someone who had the technique and the jumps and the artistry with it — not just as the artist."
KRISTI YAMAGUCHI, 1991

Yamaguchi and Nancy Kerrigan were teammates on the U.S. team in 1992 and encouraged each other through their first Olympics. They both went on to win medals.

Paul Wylie

 U.S.A.

Olympic Silver, 1992

Almost no one asked Paul Wylie for his autograph before the 1992 Olympics. But after his silver-medal finish, he became an American hero with writer's cramp! At the Olympics, Wylie showed skating fans around the world how great his skating could be. In the past he'd had trouble landing all his triple jumps in competition, but at this contest he nailed them all, and the rest of his program was nearly perfect.

Wylie skates smoothly and easily over the ice with lots of speed, and he can skate well to any type of music. The beauty of Wylie's routines makes him a favorite with any audience.

"I knew I could skate this well, but getting the medal is pure serendipity. It's especially nice because of the low expectations everyone had for me."
PAUL WYLIE, 1992

Nancy Kerrigan

U.S.A.

Olympic Silver, 1994

Olympic Bronze, 1992

Nancy Kerrigan won silver at the 1994 Olympics in one of the closest races in skating history: she skated brilliantly and missed top spot by just one-tenth of a point. She is one of the best skaters in the world because she can combine power with artistry. Kerrigan skates smoothly from one triple jump to the next and has excellent spins.

Considering what she had been through at the 1994 U.S. Nationals, Kerrigan's Olympic success was especially amazing. She suffered a knee injury after being clubbed by a "hit man" and had to miss almost three weeks of training. Thanks to the support of her family and friends, Kerrigan fought back to peak form.

"I'm going to the Olympics to do my best. I've never been more ready in my life."
NANCY KERRIGAN, 1994

Wylie and Kerrigan are good friends. They trained together and sometimes took breaks during practice and skated as a pairs team.

Golden Men

John Curry

 Great Britain

Olympic Champion, 1976

World Champion, 1976

John Curry was the first male skater from Great Britain to win Olympic gold. He had the choreography, footwork, spins and jumps of a top competitor. But what made Curry a champion was his style, which brought the grace of classical dance to the ice. Curry's ballet training made his routines smooth and graceful, and so did his ability to land his jumps lightly.

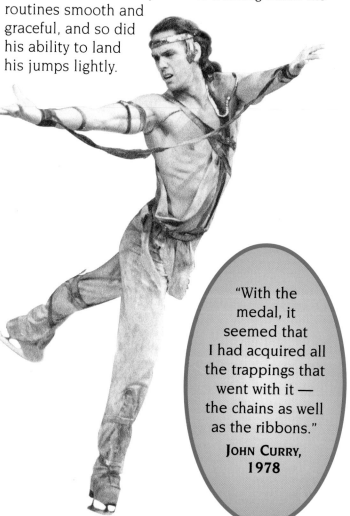

"With the medal, it seemed that I had acquired all the trappings that went with it — the chains as well as the ribbons."

JOHN CURRY, 1978

Robin Cousins

 Great Britain

Olympic Champion, 1980

Robin Cousins began skating because he wanted to be in a cool ice rink one sweltering hot day. Cousins is taller than the average male skater, and he used his long legs to lift himself into magnificent jumps. He seemed to fly effortlessly through the air. His jumps, combined with his polished routines and his ability to skate consistently in competition, made Cousins a great performer.

"Obviously you want to win, but it is always a satisfying result when you are happy with what you have done and you know that it is better than you did the last time you went on the ice."

ROBIN COUSINS, 1980

Viktor Petrenko

 Ukraine

Olympic Champion, 1992

World Champion, 1992

Viktor Petrenko is famous for his huge triple axel, which takes him far across the ice and has great height. He's also known for his sparkling personality — he makes people smile because he has fun on the ice even when he's being dramatic. Petrenko not only wins medals for his skating but he's also a champion when it comes to generosity. In 1993 he paid for skates, costumes, ice time and lessons for teammate Oksana Baiul and inspired her to win a world title.

"I have nothing to lose. It's skating and skating is my life."

VIKTOR PETRENKO, 1993

Alexei Urmanov

Russia

Olympic Champion, 1994

Winning Olympic gold in 1994 was a feat of true courage for Alexei Urmanov. In 1992 he broke his ankle when trying to land a jump and he missed six months of training. When Urmanov returned to the ice he struggled to land his quad, a jump that he'd already landed many times. He had to work hard to regain his jumps, and the injury also forced Urmanov to improve his artistry. That gave him the edge over Elvis Stojko at the 1994 Olympics and won him the gold medal.

"I just can't believe it! I am so happy!"

ALEXEI URMANOV, 1994

Perfection

Jayne Torvill & Christopher Dean

Great Britain

Olympic Champions, 1984

Olympic Bronze, 1994

World Champions, 1981–84

Jayne Torvill and Christopher Dean have earned more perfect scores of 6.0 than any skaters in the history of ice dance. After they won their first world title in 1981, Torvill and Dean were unbeatable for many years. When they entered a competition, no one doubted that they would win — the only question was how many sixes they would earn.

Smooth, innovative and clever, Torvill and Dean tell a story with their music and, like actors, they become the characters in the story. This talent allows them to take a piece of music and make it come alive. As well, Torvill and Dean stay perfectly in time with their music, and in ice dance, timing is the most important thing.

In practice and performance, Torvill and Dean are perfectionists. They can spend as long as two hours working on a move that will last only two seconds in their program. Often these moves are first created on the dance floor. Then, back on skates, Torvill and Dean flow magically through the movements.

As professionals, Torvill and Dean have skated all over the world with their own show. But the desire to compete at the 1994 Olympics brought them back to the amateur spotlight. They hadn't competed in ten years, yet they still won a bronze medal. Many thought they deserved to win gold.

Early in their careers, Torvill and Dean worked full-time and squeezed in skating practice whenever they could. Often the only time available was in the middle of the night!

Torvill and Dean are very superstitious. Dean must step on the ice with his left foot first, and Torvill has worn the same earrings — little skates — in every competition since she was 16.

Great Battles

Brian Boitano

U.S.A.

Olympic Champion, 1988

World Champion, 1986, 1988

As a kid, Brian Boitano loved to roller-skate recklessly. When he began to figure skate, he learned how to control his energy and use his power and strength to become one of the best jumpers in the sport. Not only does Boitano have some of the best jumps but he's also one of the most consistent performers.

At the 1988 Olympics, Boitano went head-to-head with Brian Orser in one of the greatest men's finals ever. It was nicknamed "the Battle of the Brians" and more television viewers tuned in for that contest than had ever watched figure skating before. With a routine that was smooth, steady and sure, Boitano thrilled the crowd with his speed and fantastic triple jumps, and won the gold in an extremely tight contest.

Boitano persuaded the International Skating Union (ISU) to let professional skaters compete at the 1994 Olympics with the amateurs. This change became known as the "Boitano Rule."

> "I would like to be known for skating when I die. I can't be unless I put it all out there on the line."
>
> **BRIAN BOITANO, 1993**

Brian Orser

Canada

Olympic Silver, 1984, 1988

World Champion, 1987

Brian Orser always looked totally relaxed and in control as a TV commentator, but at times his skating life put incredible strain on him. When he was 13, he endured the first of three broken legs in a year and a half. The second break came just after Orser qualified for his first Canadian Nationals, so he was forced to cheer from the sidelines with a broken heart.

In men's competition today, all the top skaters can land perfect triple axels. For a few years, however, Orser was the only skater who could complete them. In his jumps, Orser launches himself high into the air and rotates quickly, which gives you the impression that he's hanging in the air. He lands each jump with a deep knee bend, and that helps him maintain his speed and flow.

"Pressure is going to your job and having to do it perfectly in front of one billion people."

BRIAN ORSER, 1994

"I'm not convinced there is any consecutive five minutes in sport as lonely as a competitive figure skating program," says Orser.

Canadian Pioneers

Barbara Ann Scott

 Canada

Olympic Champion, 1948

World Champion, 1947, 1948

Barbara Ann Scott was the first North American skater to win Olympic and World gold medals. At the time she skated, competitions were held outside. Scott was a winner because she could concentrate and perform consistently despite bad weather or poor ice conditions.

Barbara Wagner & Robert Paul

 Canada

Olympic Champions, 1960

World Champions, 1957–60

In the middle of Barbara Wagner and Robert Paul's performance at the 1960 Olympics their music stopped, and they had to re-skate their routine. Despite this interruption they went on to win gold. These fast, exciting skaters set a high standard for pairs because they filled every moment of their program with interesting and difficult moves.

Donald Jackson

🇨🇦 Canada

Olympic Bronze, 1960
World Champion, 1962

Donald Jackson's life changed dramatically thanks to a last-minute decision he made at the 1962 Worlds. He was in second place going into the finals and knew that to win he had to land a triple lutz, a jump that he had landed successfully only five times in more than a thousand attempts! Jackson nailed it perfectly and took his place in history with a gold medal.

Karen Magnussen

🇨🇦 Canada

Olympic Silver, 1972
World Champion, 1973

Karen Magnussen displayed all the qualities of a champion. An athletic skater with strong jumps and good spins, she combined these elements in polished programs set to exciting music. Magnussen could also keep calm under pressure and had the ability to peak at just the right time.

Petra Burka

🇨🇦 Canada

Olympic Bronze, 1964
World Champion, 1965

After becoming World Champion in 1965, Petra Burka was voted Canadian female athlete of the year two years in a row. Burka was a consistent skater who loved to jump. In the days when few women even attempted triple jumps, she became the first woman in the world to land a triple salchow in competition.

Dynamic Duos

> "What counts is the memory of what we did, how we made the people flip out completely."
> **PAUL DUCHESNAY, 1991**

Isabelle & Paul Duchesnay

France

Olympic Silver, 1992

World Champions, 1991

This extraordinary team dared to be different. Isabelle and Paul Duchesnay challenged the rigid ice dance rules by inventing moves that were original and bold. Judges wondered whether some of their moves were even legal and had difficulty marking their routines. But the Duchesnays always captivated their audiences and they still do. Their style is to choose a theme, then put together music, costumes and choreography based on that theme. And the Duchesnays' great acting skill always makes you believe that the story they're skating is real.

The Duchesnays are Canadian but their mother is French, and that allowed them to accept an offer from France to compete on its international team.

Barbara Underhill & Paul Martini

 Canada

World Champions, 1984

When Barbara Underhill and Paul Martini became the 1984 World Champions, they won Canada's first pairs gold medal since 1962. Their program was exciting, fast and filled with strong lifts and fantastic throws. The victory felt especially good because it followed a nightmare performance at the Olympics when a slip caused Underhill and Martini to tumble and lose their chance for a medal. They wanted to quit skating forever. But then Underhill switched back to a pair of comfortable old skates, her confidence returned, and Underhill and Martini's story ended on top of the podium.

"Barbie and Paul were a joy. We all had fun every day, and through triumph and tragedy they emerged as one of the great pairs in the history of skating."

LOUIS STONG, 1995
Underhill and Martini's coach

Tracy Wilson & Rob McCall

 Canada

Olympic Bronze, 1988

Tracy Wilson and Rob McCall won an amazing seven Canadian titles in ice dance, and their 1988 Olympic bronze was the first medal ever for any Canadian dance team. Energetic and athletic, Wilson and McCall were a polished team who could transfer real ballroom dances, such as the tango, onto the ice. They were light and quick on their feet and made intricate footwork look easy. If there were two ways to perform a move, Wilson and McCall had the talent to do it the most difficult way, and that earned them top marks. Today you can see Wilson on TV commentating at major skating events.

"We wanted to bring the audience out onto the ice so that they could tap their toes along with us."

TRACY WILSON, 1994

Elegance and Style

Before her Olympic skate, Fleming pinned to her dress a lucky charm — a green gum wrapper!

Peggy Fleming

 U.S.A.

Olympic Champion, 1968

World Champion, 1966–68

When Peggy Fleming was 12, a plane heading from the United States to Czechoslovakia for the 1961 World Championships crashed, and the entire U.S. figure skating team was killed. Fleming went instantly from being a top junior to becoming the skating hope of her country.

Despite the pressure and her young age, Fleming proudly represented the U.S. at international events. A calm and shy contender, she looked delicate but was incredibly strong. In the days when athletic skating was more in style, Fleming skated with the grace of a ballet dancer, yet could match her competitors jump for jump.

Fleming now puts her skating knowledge to use on television, where she commentates at big skating competitions.

"Peggy had good jumps and more — an ethereal, elegant, feminine and graceful style presented in a quiet kind of skating. She just floated over the ice."

CAROL HEISS, 1995
Coach and former Olympic champion

Dorothy Hamill

 U.S.A.

Olympic Champion, 1976

World Champion, 1976

Often in practice Dorothy Hamill seriously doubted her skating talent and she battled her nerves at competition. But none of that insecurity ever showed. The athletic Hamill combined the whole polished package — fabulous spins, great jumps — with elegant choreography.

"Dot" is also known for inventing a spin called the Hamill Camel. It's a variation on the camel spin, in which the skater spins on one leg while the other leg is stretched out behind at 90°. When Hamill competed, she was the best spinner in the world. That could have been because of a rink she practiced on early in her career. The roof of the rink was too low to allow Hamill to jump, so she practiced her spins instead. "I did a million spins," she said.

Hamill performed the layback spin especially well.

> "I thought life would be easy afterward, until I realized my work had just begun. But if you win gold, it's a wonderful problem to have."
>
> **DOROTHY HAMILL, 1992**

"If dancing is how angels walk," says Hamill, "then skating must surely be how angels dance."

A Class by Themselves

Pairs skaters strive to match each other's movements as closely as possible, and Gordeeva and Grinkov's parallel skating was so unified that they looked like one another's shadows.

Ekaterina Gordeeva & Sergei Grinkov

Russia

Olympic Champions, 1988, 1994

World Champions, 1986, 1987, 1989, 1990

The skating world lost one of its best performers with the sudden and unexpected death of Sergei Grinkov in November 1995. Ekaterina Gordeeva and Sergei Grinkov were two of the most talented pairs skaters ever, and they seemed to skate better every time they performed.

This pair had it all: speed, power, flow and grace. When they skated, "G & G" made their spectacular throws and majestic lifts look effortless. During a jump or throw triple — a move in which the man throws his partner into the air, she rotates three times and then lands on one foot — they could maintain the same speed on the exit from the move as they had on the entry. Keeping that speed requires great skill because in order to throw his partner, the man must dig hard into the ice without going too far forward on his toe picks or they will slow him down.

In 1986, G & G won their first World Championships when "Katya" was only 14, and just two years later they struck gold at the Olympics. Gordeeva and Grinkov turned professional in 1990, but soon missed the challenge of amateur competition. Their comeback was golden when they won the 1994 Olympics. Sadly G & G will never skate together again, but the magic they created on ice lives on with Gordeeva's performances as a solo skater.

"It's just a huge shock," said pairs skater Lloyd Eisler about Grinkov's death, "and the skating world and the fans have lost someone who cannot be replaced."

"Gordeeva and Grinkov were in a league by themselves. What set them apart was their refinement, caring and tenderness for each other. They were everything pairs skating should be."
SANDRA BEZIC, 1995 Choreographer and commentator

American Gold

Tenley Albright

 U.S.A.

Olympic Champion, 1956
World Champion, 1953, 1955

Tenley Albright was the first American woman skater to win an Olympic gold medal, and she did it with a style that combined grace and strength. She was an athletic skater, but she was also ahead of her competition artistically. Albright originally began skating to strengthen her back, which had been weakened by illness when she was very young.

Carol Heiss

 U.S.A.

Olympic Champion, 1960
World Champion, 1956 – 60

Today you can see Carol Heiss at major competitions coaching her skaters. When she competed herself, she put together the best record of any woman in North America thanks to her dynamic and athletic skating. Heiss attacked her performances with lots of energy and became one of the first women to master a double axel.

Richard Button

 U.S.A.

Olympic Champion, 1948, 1952

World Champion, 1948–52

These days "Dick" Button may be more famous as a television broadcaster than as a figure skater. But he was the first American skater to win Olympic gold and the first to land both the double axel and triple loop jumps in competition. He was creative and innovative and is probably the pioneer of modern athletic skating.

Hayes Alan Jenkins

 U.S.A.

Olympic Champion, 1956

World Champion, 1953–56

Everyone in the Jenkins family loved figure skating. Hayes Alan Jenkins began by skating pairs and dance with his sister, then decided to concentrate on men's singles. His trademark was a flying sit spin, a move in which the skater leaps high into the air, then drops into a spin that's low to the ice.

David Jenkins

 U.S.A.

Olympic Champion, 1960

World Champion, 1957–59

When David Jenkins won Olympic gold, it was the first time that a brother followed a brother as Olympic champion. Jenkins was a consistent competitor and had a great ability to interpret his music. Experts claimed that he was ahead of his time because he often included triple jumps in his routines.

The Entertainers

Scott Hamilton

 U.S.A.

Olympic Champion, 1984

World Champion, 1981–84

No one has footwork like Scott Hamilton's. On the ice he is a lightning flash, with feet that move so quickly you seem to be seeing them on fast forward. He jumps and spins with ease, has enough energy to light up an arena and was born to entertain.

The road to Hamilton's success had a few obstacles. One was a childhood illness that weakened him and prevented him from growing properly. Skating helped make him strong again. Then in 1976 the cost of lessons, ice time, costumes and travel almost forced him to quit. Luckily a sponsor stepped in just in time to help.

Hamilton's career as a pro skater and TV commentator has been interrupted by cancer. No doubt he will fight the disease with the same determination he has brought to his skating.

> "Anytime you can stand at center ice and be the center of attention with the goal to entertain the audience — how can you find fault in that? It's the perfect job."
>
> **SCOTT HAMILTON, 1994**

Hamilton turned professional in 1984 and is one of the most popular skaters on the circuit. His performing ability is second to none.

Kurt Browning

![Canada flag] Canada

World Champion, 1989 – 91, 1993

Thrilling an audience goes with the name Kurt Browning. He's versatile because he can skate to any music: rock, classical, country, blues or jazz. Browning can also spin, jump and perform back flips. He's even in the *New Guinness Book of Records* for being the first skater to land a quad in competition. But it's the way he strings together his jumps, spins and footwork that really sets Browning apart.

A natural entertainer, Browning has been a showman since his very first competition, when he forgot his program and improvised. He suffered from severe back pain over the years and still tried to skate. At the 1994 Olympics Browning won the hearts of all Canadians when he apologized to his country for not doing his best. It's hard to believe that this champion took up figure skating just to improve his hockey!

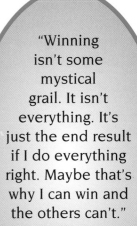

"Winning isn't some mystical grail. It isn't everything. It's just the end result if I do everything right. Maybe that's why I can win and the others can't."

KURT BROWNING, 1991

Before skating in the finals at his first World Championships in 1989, Browning told his coach that he had already accomplished a personal goal: he hadn't had a haircut for the entire season!

Unbeatable Russians

Liudmila & Oleg Protopopov

 Russia

Olympic Champions, 1964, 1968

World Champions, 1965–68

Most pairs teams start skating together in their teens, but Liudmila and Oleg Protopopov didn't team up until they were in their early twenties. Despite the late start, they soon developed into a graceful pair who skated with lots of emotion and passion. The Protopopovs were the first Russian pair to win Olympic gold. Since their win in 1964, no other country has ever won Olympic gold in pairs skating!

"The winning of gold medals for us was not so important because our goal was to express ourselves artistically ... When we could achieve that, the gold medal came by itself."

OLEG PROTOPOPOV, 1993

Irina Rodnina & Alexandr Zaitsev

 Russia

Olympic Champions, 1972*, 1976, 1980

World Champions, 1969–72*, 1973–78

(*Rodnina and Alexei Ulanov)

Irina Rodnina's record is unbeatable! With two different partners — Alexei Ulanov and Alexandr Zaitsev — this tiny but powerful pairs skater was the most dominant in the world for a decade. Rodnina and Zaitsev were well trained and consistent under pressure. They combined strong lifts, excellent side-by-side jumps and striking choreography with a competitive spirit unrivaled in figure skating.

"I don't like being second to anyone."

IRINA RODNINA, 1971

Liudmila Pakhomova & Alexander Gorshkov

 Russia

Olympic Champions, 1976
World Champions, 1970–74, 1976

Liudmila Pakhomova and Alexander Gorshkov made history when they won Olympic gold in 1976 because that was the first year that ice dance was declared an Olympic sport. Their footwork was complicated and difficult, but what really made them stand out was their elegant and dramatic style. Pakhomova and Gorshkov were one of the first dance teams to tell a story with their music when they performed.

Natalia Bestemianova & Andrei Bukin

 Russia

Olympic Champions, 1988
World Champions, 1985–88

They hit the ice and skate as if they're on fire! The success of ice dancers Natalia Bestemianova and Andrei Bukin has as much to do with their acting ability as their intricate, fast footwork and superb choreography. Bestemianova likes to use a lot of facial expression when she skates, and that makes her performance very dramatic. Some critics think she's too dramatic, but audiences are always captivated by "B & B."

"Pakhomova and Gorshkov set my inner spirit ablaze, for through their elegance, their character and their artistry I experienced pure inspiration."
BARBARA BEREZOWSKI-IVAN, 1995
Former Canadian ice dance champion

"B & B covered the ice with breakneck speed and had intensive dramatic flair. Natalia's facial expressions were amazing."
LORNA WIGHTON-ALDRIDGE, 1995
Coach and former Canadian ice dance champion

Sizzling Sophistication

Katarina Witt

 Germany

Olympic Champion, 1984, 1988

World Champion, 1984, 1985, 1987, 1988

She looks like a model, works as a television commentator and has even written her autobiography, yet Katarina Witt is most famous for her ability as a great skater. Her back-to-back Olympic golds made Witt the first woman since Sonja Henie to win gold at more than one Olympics.

Whether she skates to classical music or rock, Witt loves performing. The whole arena lights up when she skates, and her programs are a glittering combination of music, choreography and costumes.

At Worlds or the Olympics, Witt was cool under pressure and so consistent that she rarely missed a jump. Her spins were beautiful, and she covered the ice smoothly and with grace. But what was really remarkable about Witt was her ability to interpret her music. She loved to take a theme and then act out the story on the ice.

Witt turned professional in 1988 but soon missed the thrill of amateur competition. Like many pros, she got her chance to compete at the 1994 Olympics thanks to the "Boitano Rule." Skating experts wondered how Witt, who had none of the more difficult triple jumps in her program, could

In the former East Germany, where Witt grew up, she was called "Katarina the Great."

measure up to contenders who could perform
them all. But Witt knew that what she lacked in
triples, she could more than make up for in polish
and maturity.

Even though Witt didn't win a medal in 1994, she
looked like a champion and held her head high.
Her program — a moving tribute to the people of
Sarajevo, whose city has been destroyed by war —
celebrated the tenth anniversary of her 1984
Olympic victory in Sarajevo. She continues to be
one of the most popular performers in ice shows
and to compete on the pro circuit.

"To take part
in the Olympics is
the greatest thing
for an athlete."
**KATARINA WITT,
1993**

Crowd Favorites

Midori Ito

Japan

Olympic Silver, 1992

World Champion, 1990

In Japan, Midori Ito is a superstar who gets mobbed for her autograph. When you watch her skate, it's easy to see why she's a star, not just in Japan but all over the world. Ito thrills the audience with her fantastic triple jumps, and although she is only 145 cm (4 ft., 9 in.) tall, her jumps are extremely high. Ito is the finest jumper ever to burst forth in women's skating. In fact, skating star Toller Cranston commented that her jumps rival those performed by top male skaters. Ito set a record when she became the first woman to land a triple axel in competition.

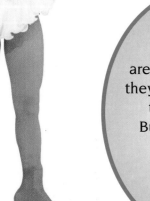

"I know some people aren't happy because they wanted me to win the gold medal. But I'm very proud of what I did."

MIDORI ITO, 1992

Ito has a dangerous habit of jumping too close to the boards. Once, after landing a jump, she fell over the barrier right into the camera pit. Later Ito found the camera operator to inquire if he was all right!

Elizabeth Manley

Canada

Olympic Silver, 1988

The 1988 Olympic Games were a dream come true for Elizabeth Manley. She delighted audiences worldwide with the performance of her life — an action-packed display of excellence including several perfect triple jumps and fabulous spins — and took home the silver medal for her great effort.

Only a few years before, a depressed and overweight Manley had quit skating. Her coaches knew that she had exceptional talent and coaxed her back to the ice. In the course of a year, she got back in shape, won silver at the Canadian championships and earned a place on the 1984 Canadian Olympic team. Her comeback was complete when she earned Olympic silver four years later.

"Liz Manley was a champion because she hit rock bottom mentally and physically, picked up the pieces and was nurtured back to her potential."

PETER DUNFIELD, 1995
Manley's coach

Philippe Candeloro

France

Olympic Bronze, 1994

When he performs, Philippe Candeloro loves to think of himself as a movie actor portraying roles on the ice. First he chooses movie music for his program, and then makes his interpretations authentic to the film script. He has fun and it shows.

Candeloro can jump high into the air and travel far across the ice. A gutsy competitor, he's also learned how to become consistent under pressure. Before skating at the 1994 Olympics, he missed 13 consecutive attempts at his triple axel, but he nailed it perfectly when he needed it the most. The effort earned Candeloro a bronze medal.

"It's very exciting when you skate on the ice and you look at the red light of the camera. When I see the red light on I look directly at it."

PHILIPPE CANDELORO, 1995

In the Spotlight

Isabelle Brasseur & Lloyd Eisler

 Canada

Olympic Bronze, 1992, 1994

World Champions, 1993

Her nickname is "Fred" and skaters know him as "Herbie." Isabelle Brasseur and Lloyd Eisler are not just immensely popular but also unbelievably talented. They perform such spectacular throws, lifts and twists that any routine they skate always brings the house down. In 1988 — their first year skating together — they earned a spot on the Canadian Olympic team.

Brasseur and Eisler's trademark move is a triple lateral twist, in which Eisler lifts Brasseur over his head, then tosses her into the air, and she rotates three times horizontally before he catches her. Because of the impact of being caught in mid-air, Brasseur cracked a rib just before the 1994 Olympics. She was in great pain while she was competing, yet she and Eisler still managed to win the bronze medal.

> "We're probably the best lifting pair in the world. And we probably have the best twists in the world."
>
> **LLOYD EISLER, 1991**

Brasseur and Eisler were the first pair to perform the triple lateral twist. They're also the only pair to do a lift called the one-handed star. In this lift, Eisler lifts Brasseur off the ice and, as you see here, holds her high over his head — all with just one hand.

Marina Klimova & Sergei Ponomarenko

Russia

Olympic Champions, 1992

World Champions, 1989, 1990, 1992

The elegant and romantic Marina Klimova and Sergei Ponomarenko can perform in many styles, anything from dreamy and romantic to lively and comical. And this dance team does it all with a technical ability that is first-rate. Klimova and Ponomarenko combine lightning-fast footwork with smooth skating and cover the ice easily from end to end. They're similar in size, which helps add to the impression that they're two bodies moving as one.

Klimova and Ponomarenko won Worlds two years in a row and then came second in 1991. Not being in first place made them determined to improve, and they practiced long hours to add new and difficult moves to their program. The hard work paid off when the gold was theirs again in 1992.

"We have different programs and different styles each year. We can skate in fun or tragic."

SERGEI PONOMARENKO, 1986

Klimova and Ponomarenko are the only skaters in ice dance history to win every color of medal at the Olympics: bronze in 1984, silver in 1988 and gold in 1992.

The Innovator

Cranston had the best Russian split jumps in the world when he was competing.

Toller Cranston

Canada

Olympic Bronze, 1976

Canadian Champion, 1971–76

Few skaters have had as much impact on figure skating as Toller Cranston. His jumps, spins and footwork were great, but how he presented them was what really set him apart. He used his entire body to interpret his music, and skating was never the same. After his brilliant skate in the finals at the 1974 World Championships in Munich, one newspaper declared him the "skater of the century."

Some people, including a few of the skating authorities, thought his ideas were weird, but Cranston created moves that had never been seen before. For instance, in a sit spin, the skater spins in a sitting position with one leg straight out in front. But halfway through Cranston's spin he would suddenly change positions and place his leg in a bent position to the side. His original and innovative move was eventually called the broken leg sit spin. Other Cranston innovations came in the form of music, costumes and drama. He skated to music from operas before anyone else, and he once even performed in a straitjacket, pretending to be insane. Cranston was also the first skater who pretended to "die" at the end of a routine. Soon

At the height of his career Cranston was such a crowd favorite that he would often be called back to do ten encores in a show.

"I craved to be different and I was different. And I wasn't afraid to show it."

**TOLLER CRANSTON,
1995**

skaters everywhere were lying down and sliding across the ice. Once any of his moves were copied, Cranston would create others so that his programs remained unique.

Cranston continues to be a favorite at ice shows and is also an outspoken skating commentator on television. As well, he is a painter, and the works he creates are colorful and intricate. Cranston's imagination is always filled with ideas for his work on and off the ice.

Contenders and Defenders

Michelle Kwan

 U.S.A.

World Champion, 1996

In 1994, when she was 13 and the youngest American competitor ever to compete at Worlds, Michelle Kwan amazed the crowd by popping off five perfect triple jumps. "Little Kwan" flows gracefully from one end of the ice to the other and is working hard to add the most difficult triple to her program — the axel. If Kwan can continue to develop her strength and maintain her consistency in competition, then Olympic gold could be in her future.

"There is really no limit to what Michelle is capable of when she gets physically stronger. She's a smart and disciplined athlete with an artistic soul."

LORI NICHOL, 1995
Kwan's choreographer

Todd Eldredge

 U.S.A.

World Champion, 1996

His speed, jumps and smoothness catapulted Todd Eldredge to a pair of U.S. National titles in the early 1990s. Then, plagued by injuries and inconsistency, Eldredge fell from first to worst with a losing streak that would have finished a weaker athlete. But Eldredge refused to give up, and his hard work earned him a gold medal at Worlds in 1996.

"The story of his life is like his jumps: now matter how tough or off-kilter things might get, he lands upright on a strong edge."

DICK BUTTON, 1997

Oksana Gritschuk & Evgeny Platov

Russia

Olympic Champions, 1994

World Champions, 1994 – 1997

With their modern style and a program set to rock and roll music, the energetic Oksana Gritschuk and Evgeny Platov grabbed Olympic gold in 1994. These attractive dancers cover the ice quickly and have non-stop energy. Crowds like them because they have lots of personality, they look as if they love performing and they choose music that is well known and upbeat.

Jenni Meno & Todd Sand

U.S.A.

U.S. National Champions, 1994 – 1996

Jenni Meno and Todd Sand look like magic on ice because they've mastered the most important skill in pairs skating: the ability to skate as one person. They also combine grace with tremendous speed, majestic lifts and athletic throws. If they can remain injury-free and be consistent in competition, this pair could earn a medal at the 1998 Olympics.

"They've created their own elegant, classical, balletic style which we don't see very much of these days."

JOHN NICKS, 1994
Meno and Sand's coach

"They can show not only the style for today but for tomorrow and after tomorrow — easy, light, natural, modern and classical."

NATALIA LINICHUK, 1993
Gritschuk and Platov's coach

The Future

Tara Lipinski

 U.S.A.

World Champion, 1997

Tara Lipinski made skating history not only when she became both the youngest U.S. National and World Champion at age 14, but also as the first woman to land a triple-loop–triple-loop combination in competition. Even though she's tiny, "Leaping Lipinski" has incredible jumps, which she combines with great spins and beautiful moves.

"Being the youngest [World Champion] is a great accomplishment. It sets a record, but I think whatever age you are, you're happy with what you get."
TARA LIPINSKI, 1997

Shae-Lynn Bourne & Victor Kraatz

 Canada

Canadian Champions, 1993–97

Shae-Lynn Bourne and Victor Kraatz did something that's almost impossible for ice dancers. At the 199 Worlds they came 14th, then jumped to 6th in 1994 4th in 1995 and 3rd in 1996 and 1997. Dancers rarel move that quickly up the rankings. But Bourne and Kraatz made such incredible progress because of their smooth skating and innovative moves. These include hydroblading, in which both their bodies ar horizontal to the ice. Watch for them on the 1998 Olympic podium.

"Every move and every step we practice each day, we do with one goal in mind: to win gold."
VICTOR KRAATZ, 1995